P9-CJX-856

*Hollie Nelson*
*Mis Tyser*
*clase*

# Table of Contents

# Chapter 1:
# Seeing Stars

"Heel, boy!" Olivia called as she ran across town.

A happy brown puppy was scampering ahead of her. When he heard Olivia's voice, he stopped and wagged his tail. He had been chasing a butterfly.

Olivia laughed and bent down to pet him. "Good boy!" she said. A gray kitty on her shoulder purred. She patted her, also. "You, too, Maxie."

Helping her aunt Sophie train pets for the local vet clinic was Olivia's second-favorite thing about her new home in Heartlake City.

Her favorite thing? That was easy. Olivia loved hanging out with her four best friends—Stephanie, Andrea, Mia, and Emma. In fact, she was on her way to meet them right now.

"Hi, Olivia!" Mia called from a bench when Olivia reached the park. "I got here early to watch the people riding horses on the trails."

Olivia smiled. That was typical of Mia. She loved animals of all kinds and even had her own horse named Bella.

"How's the pet training going?" Mia asked.

Before Olivia could answer, Stephanie and Emma hurried over to join them. "Hi, guys!" Stephanie exclaimed. "Sorry we're late. We would have been here on time. But *someone* had to stop and look at the new headbands at the boutique."

"What?" Emma shrugged, adjusting a pretty purple headband in her perfectly brushed hair. "The new season's styles just came out. Besides, Andrea's not even here yet."

"Maybe she's working on a new song," Olivia said. "I think Marie is letting her sing at the café every Friday this month."

The girls all nodded. Their friend Andrea was a fantastic singer. She worked during the summer as a waitress at the City Park Café and spent most of her time dreaming up new song lyrics. The café's owner, Marie, didn't mind as long as the food orders came out right. Everyone in town knew Andrea's dream was to become a big star one day.

Just then, Andrea came sprinting up to the

bench. She was out of breath. "You guys . . . never . . . believe . . . saw." She panted.

"Slow down." Stephanie laughed. "We can't understand you."

Andrea took a deep breath. "What I meant was, you guys will never believe who I just saw!" she said. "Look over there!"

Andrea pointed to a woman riding a horse near the edge of the woods.

Mia giggled. "There are always people riding horses in the afternoon, silly," she said.

"Forget the horse—look at the *rider*," Andrea insisted. "Isn't that . . . *Cassie*?"

Emma gasped. "Cassie? You mean *the* Cassie—as in the host of *Girl Power*?"

"That's my favorite TV show!" Stephanie cried.

"What's Cassie doing here?" Olivia wondered.

"I don't know, but let's go ask for her autograph!" Andrea exclaimed.

The five girls raced to the other side of the park.

But before they could get there, Cassie turned her horse onto a trail and cantered out of sight.

"Oh, no! There's no way we can catch up to her on foot!" Andrea groaned.

Emma frowned. "Then how are we going to find her?"

"We need to figure out what she's doing in Heartlake City," Stephanie declared. "Come on, I have an idea."

# Chapter 2:
# The Contest

Soon the friends were sitting in Stephanie's backyard. Even Stephanie's cat, Kitty, could tell something big was going on. She wandered into the yard and circled the girls' feet.

"Okay," Stephanie said. "Emma, you look through the Heartlake City newspaper and see what's going on around town. And, Mia, you turn on the radio. If Cassie's here for her television show, maybe there will be an announcement."

Olivia smiled. *Leave it to Stephanie to take charge of the situation!* she thought.

Mia turned on the radio. A pop song was just finishing.

"*Goooood* morning, Heartlake City!" The DJ's voice came on. "We've got big news to share today. Some of you may have noticed a special visitor around town. Cassie, the host of the television show *Girl Power*, is here!"

"It *was* her!" Emma exclaimed, jumping up and down eagerly.

"*Ssh!* Maybe he'll explain why she's visiting," Olivia said, leaning closer to the radio.

"Now, fans, Cassie has just announced an exciting contest," the DJ continued. "She is so impressed by our beautiful city that she wants to feature it on an episode of *Girl Power*. And one lucky girl has the chance to win a guest-star appearance on the show!"

"Wow!" Stephanie cried. "That sounds like it would be amazing!"

"Definitely," Andrea said. "I was *made* to be on TV. If I win, maybe I can sing with Cassie."

"The contest theme is *The Heart of Heartlake City*," the DJ said. "Whichever girl submits the most creative entry—from photos to videos to scrapbooks—about what makes our city special will win the grand prize. All entries are due at City Hall by five o'clock on Friday afternoon. That's four days away. So get to work, girls!"

As the pop music started back up, Stephanie clapped her hands. "This is going to be awesome!"

"We should enter together!" Olivia cried.

"Yeah!" her friends agreed.

"Wait a second," Mia said suddenly. "Didn't the DJ say only *one* girl could win?"

"You're right." Emma's face fell. "I guess we're not allowed to enter as a group."

"Oh." Olivia sighed. "That's too bad. We could have made the best entry *ever*."

"I know." Stephanie shrugged. "We should all still enter, though. That will give us five chances to win. Maybe at least one of us will get to meet Cassie."

Andrea nodded. "And then I—um, I mean, *whoever* wins can tell the rest of us all about it."

"Okay," Olivia said. She still felt disappointed. But she didn't want to spoil her friends' excitement. "What should our projects be?"

Stephanie grinned. "I know what I'm going to do. Wait here!" She ran inside her house.

"I think I'll do something about Heartlake City's animals," Mia said.

"Of course!" Emma exclaimed. "That's perfect.

Heartlake is special to you because of the animals."

"What about you, Emma?" Olivia asked.

"I'll probably do something about fashion," Emma said, twirling a strand of her hair. "I can take photos of great outfits and write about them. It will be like a Heartlake City fashion magazine."

"And I'm going to write my very own song," Andrea announced. "What about you, Olivia?"

"I'm not sure," Olivia said.

Just then, Stephanie returned holding a book.

"What's that?" Mia asked.

"It's a book about the history of Heartlake City," Stephanie explained. "I need it to research my *own* book."

Emma gasped. "You're going to write a *whole* book by Friday?"

"Wow!" Olivia exclaimed. That sounded like a lot of work. But if anyone could do it, it was Stephanie.

Stephanie smiled. "This book only talks about

old stuff that happened here," she said, flipping through the pages. "I want my book to be about stuff that's happening now. Like all the fun things there are to see and do around town."

"That's really cool." Olivia looked around at her friends. "All of your projects sound amazing. I bet Cassie will have a hard time picking a winner."

Mia nodded. "But you still need to think of a project to do, Olivia."

Olivia shrugged. "Don't worry about me. I'll keep brainstorming. For now, I'm happy to help you guys out with your ideas."

"Okay." Andrea grinned. "Well, then, may the best girl win!"

# Chapter 3:
# Write On,
# Stephanie!

As soon as Stephanie's friends left, she started scribbling down an outline.

"I can write a chapter about the beach," she murmured to herself. "And another about our school, and the shops and restaurants downtown."

She picked up the history book and flipped through it.

What else should she write about?

"I'd better go out and do some research," she told Kitty. "Wish me luck!"

The cat purred as Stephanie gave her a pat. Then Stephanie hurried off.

Stephanie spent the rest of the day wandering around town, jotting ideas in her notebook. Soon, she had collected details about the stables, the flight school, the café, the pet salon, and even the Heartlake City Pool. By that evening, she was exhausted!

Tuesday morning, Stephanie headed to the park. It was beautiful outside, and she wanted to organize her notes for the first few chapters in the bright sunshine. When she got there, Mia was sitting on their usual bench, taking photos of horses cantering along the trails.

"Hi," Mia called. "How's the book going?"

"Great," Stephanie said. "How's your project?"

Mia sighed. "Actually, it's harder than I thought," she confessed. "I've been taking photos of cute animals all morning. But I'm not sure how to turn them into a project Cassie will like."

"Don't worry, you'll figure it out," Stephanie assured her. "I know you can do it!"

"Thanks," Mia said. "Actually, the one I'm really worried about is Olivia. When I talked to her this morning, she still didn't know what she's doing."

"Olivia's supersmart," Stephanie pointed out. "She's always inventing cool science projects. She

will probably do something about science that will show Cassie how smart Heartlake City girls are."

"I didn't think of that," Mia said.

Suddenly, Andrea ran up to them. She was clutching some papers and looked excited.

"Guess what?" Andrea said breathlessly. "I'm going to sing my song for the contest at the café on Thursday afternoon! Will you guys help me tape it for Cassie?"

"Of course!" Stephanie and Mia exclaimed.

"Fabulous!" Andrea waved the papers she was holding. "I have some of the lyrics worked out already. Olivia has been helping me with the

rhymes." She squinted at the paper. "I just wish she'd helped me with my handwriting. I can hardly read what I wrote."

Stephanie giggled. "Great artists don't always have good handwriting."

"True." Andrea grinned. "Speaking of writing, how's your book going?"

"It's all under control," Stephanie said. "Almost, anyway." She frowned and wiggled her fingers. "My hand hurts from all the writing."

"You're *hand*writing your book?" Mia asked, surprised. "How come you're not using a computer?"

Stephanie smiled. "Oh, don't worry. I'm only handwriting my notes. For the book itself, I know just what to do."

A short while later, Stephanie ran up to her dad's study at home. "Hey, Dad," she said, rushing in. "May I borrow your laptop?"

Her father looked up from his desk. "Sorry, Steph. It's not working right now. It keeps freezing every time I load a video or computer game. I need to have it repaired."

"I don't need to play games," Stephanie said. "I only need it to write my book."

"Oh. It should work okay for that if you're careful." He placed the old laptop on his desk. Stephanie turned it on and held her breath.

"Yes!" she exclaimed when the screen lit up. It worked! With all her notes, Stephanie was certain she could finish her book by Friday.

*Maybe, just maybe*, she thought, *I will be the one to win the contest!*

# Chapter 4: Picture-Perfect Emma

"Now stay just like that," Emma said, looking through her camera lens.

"Like this?" Olivia struck a pose. It was Wednesday morning, and she was standing in Emma's backyard. Her friend had asked each of the girls to be in her Heartlake City fashion shoot.

Emma snapped the picture. "Perfect! Thanks for helping me. What's your project, by the way?"

Olivia sighed. "I'm still not sure. I thought about doing something about science, but I couldn't figure out how to make it go with the theme of the contest."

"You'd better hurry up and decide," Emma said, her face growing serious. "The deadline is only two days away."

Just then Mia came into the yard. She was holding a cute bunny in her arms. "I'm here!" she said. "And I brought Fluffy, just like you asked."

"Perfect!" Emma exclaimed. "Since you love animals so much, a photo shoot wouldn't be you without a cute animal in it, too!"

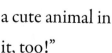

Emma took lots of photos of Mia posing with the rabbit. Then she asked Mia and Olivia to pose together. All the pictures were turning out great!

Later, Emma met up with Stephanie at the park for her photo session. "Sorry I'm late," Emma said. "I stopped to take pictures of some fashionable clothes I saw in a store window on the way here."

"It's okay." Stephanie set down her laptop. "I was working on my book."

"Are you ready to be a fashion model?" Emma asked, smiling.

Stephanie and Emma walked over to a trail at the edge of the woods. "These trees will make a good background," Emma said. She held up her hands, pretending to look through a camera lens. "But the sun needs to be behind me when I take your picture."

"Okay. How about this?" Stephanie stepped off the trail and struck a pose.

"Freeze right there!" Emma backed up, still holding her hands up to frame the shot.

"That looks perfect. One second. Just let me grab my camer—*aah*!"

Emma cried out and jumped aside as loud hoofbeats pounded up behind her. A second later, a white horse crashed out of the bushes.

"Snowball, whoa!" a familiar voice cried.

"Mia!" Stephanie exclaimed. "What are you doing here?"

Mia calmed the horse. Then she slid down from the saddle. "The stable owner asked me to exercise her new horse, so I brought her out here on the riding trail," she said with a frown. "What are you two doing here? I thought you were doing all the photo shoots in your backyard. You shouldn't stand on the trails like that!"

"Sorry," Emma said. "But I wanted to take some pictures of Stephanie in the park. You and Snowball scared us, too, you know."

"Oh." Mia looked down. "I guess you're right. Sorry I got mad."

Emma relaxed. She didn't mean to yell at her friend. "That's okay. You're right; we shouldn't have been standing on the trails. But now that you're here, how about a few photos together? You, Stephanie, and Snowball in a riding shot will be the perfect way to finish my fashion shoot of Heartlake City!"

As the shutter on Emma's camera clicked with each shot, her smile grew a little wider. *This is going perfectly*, she thought to herself. *Cassie will think this is the most creative—and fashionable—entry for sure!*

# Chapter 5:
# Mia's Animal Surprise

\* \* \*

"Good girl, Snowball." Mia said later that afternoon as she led the horse into its stable. "Enjoy your hay."

Mia sighed as Snowball began munching. Seeing her friends in the park had reminded Mia that she needed to figure out a way to make her photos of animals work for the contest, too.

So far, she had lots of pictures of horses, cats, dogs, and birds around town.

The trouble was, none of the pictures seemed exciting enough to impress Cassie. "Emma's fashion shoot makes sense," Mia said. "But somehow, a scrapbook of animals doesn't seem as exciting."

Just then, the sound of hoofbeats distracted her. Mia walked toward the practice ring. Her riding teacher, Freya, was there on her horse.

Freya's boyfriend was watching from inside the barn. And behind his back, Mia could see he was holding flowers for Freya. But unbeknownst to him, a hungry horse was sniffing at them curiously!

"Oh!" Mia whispered to herself. "That's too funny!" She tiptoed closer and took several photos of the pair. Then she looked at her pictures.

Somehow they just didn't seem to capture the heart of the moment.

"There's got to be a way to really show how special all the animals make Heartlake City." Mia sighed. "Maybe Olivia's aunt, Sophie, will have some advice. She works with animals all day. She might know what to do."

When Mia arrived at the Heartlake City Vet, Aunt Sophie was standing outside.

"Hi," Mia called. "Can I ask you something?"

"Sure, Mia," Aunt Sophie replied. "I was just letting Freddy get some fresh air. Let's go inside."

"Freddy?" Mia repeated. "Who's Freddy?"

Suddenly, something small and hairy leaped in front of Mia, chattering with excitement. It looked like a fuzzy little person! Mia was so startled that she jumped into Aunt Sophie's arms.

Aunt Sophie laughed. "*That's* Freddy," she explained. "He's a baby chimp from the zoo."

"Oh!" Mia grinned, feeling sheepish. "He's . . . um . . . cute."

"And mischievous. We'd better bring him back inside," Aunt Sophie said.

Mia was helping to put Freddy back in his cage when Olivia arrived at the clinic. "Aw, what a cute chimp!" she said.

"Yeah," Mia agreed, handing Freddy a toy to play with. The little chimp eagerly grabbed it and began chewing on it. "You should have been here earlier," Mia said. She told Olivia about Freddy startling her. "I'll bet it looked hilarious when I jumped into your aunt's arms! Too bad nobody was here to take a picture for my project."

Olivia grinned. "Too bad nobody was here with a video camera." Her eyes widened. "Hey, that gives me a great idea. Why don't you do a movie about animals instead of just photos?"

Mia gasped. "Olivia, you're a genius!" she cried. "That's the perfect way to make my project special. I'm sure I can get lots of great video of Heartlake City's animals!" She paused. "But wait—you're so good at technical stuff. And it was your idea. Don't you want to do a movie as *your* project?"

Olivia shrugged. "That could be fun," she said, looking down. "But even if I end up doing a movie, it won't be focused on animals like yours. So go ahead!"

"Great! Thanks a bunch for the idea!" Mia grabbed Olivia in a big hug. "I'd better go home and borrow my dad's video camera. I've got some catching up to do!"

# Chapter 6: Olivia on Her Own

After Mia left, Aunt Sophie turned to her niece. She could tell something was wrong. "Olivia, shouldn't you be working on your own project?" she asked. "I've been hearing about the contest from my clients all week. It sounds like every girl in Heartlake City is entering."

*Every girl except me*, Olivia thought sadly.

"I haven't come up with a good enough idea yet," Olivia said softly.

Aunt Sophie raised an eyebrow.

"But the deadline is Friday afternoon, isn't it?" she asked. "Sweetie, what's wrong? Why don't you want to enter the contest?"

Olivia sighed. "I still feel kind of new in town," she said. "All my friends have such great ideas. But every time I ask myself what I like about living in Heartlake City, all I can think of is how much I enjoy hanging out with them." Olivia shrugged. "I can't really make an entry about that, can I?"

Aunt Sophie put her arm around Olivia. "You know what I think?" she said. "I think you can make an entry about whatever you want. You should talk to Mia and the other girls. Maybe they're having the same thought, and you guys can enter together."

Olivia shook her head. "No, we can't. Only one girl can win the contest. It said so in the rules." She took a deep breath. "It's okay. Emma, Stephanie, Mia, and Andrea's projects are all so cool. I'm sure one of them will win. And I've been helping them. So that's almost as good as winning, right?"

*** 

That night, Olivia changed into her pajamas and flopped onto her bed. She was still thinking about what her aunt had said.

The little puppy she was training hopped around the edge of the bed. "Sit!" Olivia told him. The dog flopped onto the floor and wagged his tail. "Good boy." Olivia smiled.

She patted the dog's head. "I wish we could have all entered together," she said. "I know we could have come up with the winning entry." She reached over to her nightstand and picked up a picture she had taken with Emma, Stephanie, Andrea, and Mia earlier that summer. They were all smiling and laughing in the photo.

"What I love about Heartlake City are my friends.

That's what makes it special to me," she said quietly.

As Olivia looked at the picture, an idea slowly began to form in her mind. It was a great idea. A *winning* idea.

*Bong!* Suddenly, the clock chimed. Olivia jumped, startled. It was ten o'clock on Wednesday night. There was only a day and a half left until contest entries were due!

Olivia sighed. There wasn't enough time to start a new entry now. After all, her friends were all almost done with their projects.

She rolled over to go to sleep. Like Olivia had told her aunt, she was sure one of her friends would win. That was good enough for her.

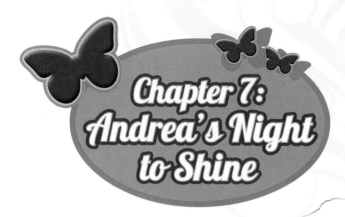

# Chapter 7:
# Andrea's Night
# to Shine

*"Do re mi fa so la ti do!"* Andrea sang.

*"Whoo!"* Olivia cheered. "Sounding great, A!"

It was Thursday afternoon, and all four of Andrea's friends were at the café for her big performance. Olivia and Emma were sipping cocoa while Mia and Stephanie were working on their laptops.

"I'm just warming up, silly," Andrea said with a smile. "You don't have to cheer yet."

Olivia shrugged. "Well, I still think you sound great." Then she turned to Emma. "Doesn't she?"

"What?" Emma asked, looking distracted.

Olivia frowned. "Are you okay, Emma? You've been really quiet."

Emma was about to reply when Marie, the café owner, rushed over.

"The camera is ready to go!" she exclaimed.

Andrea looked over at the movie camera at the edge of the café and clapped with excitement. When Marie had heard about Andrea's project, she had

offered to record Andrea on her old-fashioned film-reel camera, straight from Hollywood! It was perfect. Anyone could take a digital video of themselves. But this motion-picture film would make it extra glamorous. When Cassie received the Hollywood-style movie of Andrea singing her special song about Heartlake City, it was sure to stand out as the winning entry!

Andrea nodded. "I'm ready."

She held up her microphone and took a deep breath. Marie started the music.

*"No matter how far I roam,"* Andrea sang, *"Heartlake City is my home . . ."*

"Woo-hoo!" her friends cheered loudly. "You go, girl!"

*"And I work part-time at the café,"* Andrea sang. *"Is it a great place? All I can say is—"*

Andrea looked over to Marie. Suddenly, she noticed a woman sitting at the back table. It was . . . Cassie!

"No way!" Andrea exclaimed.

"Huh?" Marie said with a frown. Andrea's friends looked surprised, too.

Andrea gulped. She'd just messed up. Big time. She had turned the line "hip hip hooray" into "no way." So it had sounded like she didn't like working at the café! And Cassie was actually there, watching her performance live!

*"I mean, uh, hooray?"* she sang weakly.

"Um . . ." She tried to remember the next line of the song. *"Uh, then there's our beautiful Heartlake Park, where we always hang out from dawn until dark . . ."*

Andrea managed to finish the song without any other mistakes. When the last note finished and the lights came up, Andrea glanced over to where Cassie had been sitting. But the television host had left.

"Oh, no!" Andrea blurted out. "She's gone!

"Who's gone?" Stephanie asked.

"Cassie!" Andrea told her friends what she'd seen.

"Oh, wow, Cassie was here?" Emma exclaimed.

"It's okay," Olivia said, patting Andrea's shoulder. "I know you messed up a bit. But you can record it again so it's perfect for the contest."

"Yeah," Stephanie agreed. "Cassie's in show business herself. She'll understand."

That made Andrea feel a little better. Hopefully, there was enough old-style film to record her song one more time.

Suddenly, her eyes grew wide.

"What's that cat doing over by the camera?" she exclaimed.

Marie looked over and gasped. "Oh, no!" she cried. She picked up the kitten, who was completely tangled in the film!

"She must have thought the film was a toy," Marie moaned. "She's pulled out the whole roll! It's all gone. How can we record more now?"

# Chapter 8:
# A Friendly
# Idea

"Can you fix it?" Andrea asked anxiously.

"I don't think so," Olivia said. "Film gets ruined when it's exposed to light. You'll need a new roll."

Marie shook her head. "It's not easy to find that kind of film. It will take a week to order more."

"A week?" Andrea cried. "But the contest deadline is tomorrow!"

"It's okay." Mia put an arm around Andrea. "I can film you with my digital camera."

"Thanks." Andrea sighed. But it just didn't feel the same.

"Here," Mia said. "Let me save my movie and we can set up to rerecord your song."

Mia opened her laptop. "Actually, Olivia, I could use your help," she said. "This video software has been giving me problems all day. I can upload and play a video, but I can't edit it. Watch."

The friends looked over Mia's shoulder as she played a funny clip of a horse pushing a rider into a haystack. "See?" she told Olivia. "I can play it, but it won't let me add it to my other clips."

"That video is hilarious!" Stephanie exclaimed. "Can you e-mail it to me?"

"Sure," Mia said. She clicked a few more keys.

Stephanie opened her laptop. "Let me see if it came through." Her fingers flew over the keys. "There it is!" She laughed as the clip began to play. Then, suddenly, she gasped.

"What's wrong?" Olivia asked.

"Oh, no! No, no, no!" Stephanie started hitting keys. "I think the video just froze up my laptop. And the entire manuscript for my book is on here!"

Her friends rushed over. But none of them could figure out how to fix the problem.

"I think that video crashed the hard drive," Olivia said at last.

"I'm so sorry, Stephanie!" Mia exclaimed.

Stephanie shook her head. "It's not your fault, it's mine. My dad warned me this computer wasn't working very well."

"This is a disaster!" Andrea exclaimed. "First I mess up my lyrics, and my film gets ruined. Then Mia's program won't work. And now Stephanie just lost her book! Nothing is going right today."

"Yeah. I guess Emma's the only one of us who can win now," Mia said.

Emma winced. "Don't count on it," she said. "I didn't tell you guys before because I didn't want to spoil Andrea's big night, but my fashion scrapbook is ruined." Her green eyes filled with tears. "I glued all the photos in last night. But something went wrong. This morning, the glue had seeped through. The pages are all stuck together and the pictures are a mess. That scrapbook took me all night to put together. I can't make another one in time."

"Don't panic, everyone," Olivia said. "We'll figure something out."

"It's too late," Andrea told her. "I'm already panicking."

"No, listen," Olivia said. "We can't give up now."

Mia shook her head. "Thanks, Olivia. But there's just not enough time to fix all four of our projects before the deadline. Not even with all of us working together."

What Mia said reminded Olivia of her project idea from last night. And slowly, she started to realize that not only was it the right project, but it was the *only* project that could work. "There might not be enough time to fix *four* projects," Olivia said slowly. "But I bet we can finish *one* project in plenty of time!"

"*One* project?" Andrea echoed.

Olivia nodded. "I think we should put all of our ideas together and enter as a team, with a project about *friendship*."

"A project about friendship?" Stephanie said. "What do you mean?"

"It's the only thing that makes sense," Olivia explained. "We're supposed to capture the heart of Heartlake City, right? Well, the heart of Heartlake City is *us*." Olivia threw her arms out. "Our friendship has been the perfect entry all along!"

"Maybe that's the reason none of our projects worked out right," Stephanie said thoughtfully. "I could have used all of your advice on what to include in my book."

"And my video would have been better with Emma's artistic eye helping me," Mia added.

"And if Stephanie was helping me with my scrapbook, I'm sure I wouldn't have glued the photos in wrong," Emma said.

Andrea put her arm around Olivia. "The only reason my song turned out so awesome is because Olivia helped with the lyrics."

Emma looked confused. "But wait, we can't enter together, can we? The contest said only *one* girl could win."

"I know." Olivia shrugged. "And maybe that means we won't win. But at least we'll have a chance to show Cassie what's most important to *these* Heartlake City girls. Besides, it'll be fun! What do you say?"

"Let's do it!" the girls cheered.

## Chapter 9: We Can Do It!

The next day was very busy for the five friends. There was a lot to do if they wanted to finish their combined project before the deadline!

As usual, Stephanie took charge of the planning. "This is going to be a multimedia project about our friendship and what we do together in Heartlake City," she said. "That means we'll need photos, video, music, and more."

"Cool," Emma said. "We're good at all that stuff."

"I know." Stephanie smiled. "We'll definitely want to use the fashion photos you have left over that you took of us, to show how you keep us looking stylish!"

"And Andrea's song," Mia put in.

"I can add in lyrics about each of us," Andrea piped up.

Olivia nodded. "And we have Mia's video footage of the animals. I asked my parents if I could borrow their new laptop, and it works great. I'll be able to edit it in no time."

"Perfect," Stephanie said. "And I still have some handwritten notes from my book. I can record voiceover of some of what I wrote and add in parts about each of us to our presentation."

"Let's get started!" Andrea exclaimed.

The girls got to work.

Andrea changed into a pretty dress, and Stephanie helped her record her song. Then Andrea helped Stephanie tape her voiceover.

Meanwhile, Emma made sure everyone's outfits looked perfect. Olivia figured out how to set Emma's camera to take pictures with a remote control. That way, they all got to pose together on the shore of Lake Heart.

"Now what?" Mia asked.

"We already have lots of videos of horses," Stephanie said. "But our best rider isn't in any of them." She pointed at Mia.

"You're right." Emma grabbed Mia's camera. "Come on, let's go to the stable. It's time for another video shoot!"

They all rushed to the Heartlake Stables. The girls took video of Mia riding while cheering her on, just like in a real competition!

"This is great!" Olivia exclaimed. "We've got Andrea's song for music, Emma's photos of us,

Stephanie's narration, and Mia's riding video for sports. What else?"

Stephanie tapped her chin. "I think the last thing we need," she said with a smile, "is an ending recorded by our very own Olivia."

"Me?" Olivia asked surprised.

"Yes, you!" Stephanie exclaimed. "Without you, none of us would have thought of this. It was your idea how our friendship is the heart of Heartlake City. I think you should record the ending to the presentation!"

Olivia couldn't stop smiling as her friends all gathered around her. Mia quickly set up the video camera, and the girls stood side by side as the red recording light blinked on.

"What is the 'heart' of Heartlake City for me?" Olivia began. "When I first moved here, everyone told me the town was special. All the buildings were beautiful. All the people were friendly. And my aunt Sophie said it was the perfect place to live.

"But there was something missing. That is, until I met my four best friends. Now, I always know I have someone I can count on, no matter what. Whether I'm training puppies in the park, studying for school, hanging out at the café, or having a sleepover in my tree house, I wouldn't want to do any of it without my friends.

"For me, the best part of our town is the friends I've made here. Heartlake City is a special place to live. But my friends make it home.

"And what more could I ask for than that?"

# Chapter 10: And the Winners Are...

＊＊＊

On Monday, the five friends gathered at Stephanie's house again. "The mayor is supposed to announce the winner of the contest in ten minutes," Stephanie said.

Andrea crossed her fingers. "I hope we win!"

"It's okay even if we don't," Olivia reminded the others. "Remember, the contest was supposed to be for one girl. We might get disqualified."

"But that's okay." Mia smiled. "It was fun anyway!"

Just then the phone rang.

Stephanie ran to answer it.

"Hello?" she said. "This is Stephanie."

"Well, hello, young lady." The mayor's familiar voice came over the receiver. "I'm glad I caught you. I have terrific news!"

"Really?" Stephanie clutched the phone tightly.

"You won the contest! Congratulations!"

"We won?" Stephanie repeated in disbelief.

"We won!" her friends all cried at once. They jumped up and hugged one another.

The mayor continued speaking on the other end of the line. Stephanie was so excited she could barely listen to what he was saying.

"Cassie was so impressed that she'd love to meet you," the mayor said. "Here's her address."

Stephanie quickly wrote it down and thanked the mayor before hanging up. Then she turned back to her friends. "I can't believe it!" she exclaimed, waving Cassie's address in the air. "She wants to meet us!"

Her friends all laughed and shouted.

Their entry had worked. They'd won!

Suddenly, Mia stopped. "Wait a minute," she said. "Cassie knows all of us entered together, right?"

Stephanie grew quiet. "I'm not sure," she said. "There was only room on the entry form to write one name. But I put a little star next to my name and wrote the rest of your names on the back."

"Do you think Cassie saw the other names?" Emma asked.

Andrea shrugged. "There's only one way to find out. Let's go meet her!"

"I'm so nervous!" Olivia exclaimed, staring up at the mansion in front of them.

Stephanie checked the address one more time. "This is the place."

The girls walked through the large front gate and knocked on the heavy wooden door. It swung open . . . and there was Cassie!

"Wow!" Stephanie exclaimed. "It's really you!"

"You must be Stephanie," Cassie said with a warm smile. "Welcome."

"Thanks," Stephanie said, sounding almost as confident as usual. "Um, and these are my friends Olivia, Andrea, Emma, and Mia. We entered your contest—all five of us—as a team."

"Yeah," Emma added. "We're best friends."

"Your contest rules said we were supposed to be creative," Mia said.

"And capture the heart of Heartlake City," Andrea added.

"Well, we're the most creative when we work together, and our friendship is what's special to us about Heartlake City," Olivia finished. She held her breath as Cassie looked them over, one by one. Would she disqualify them?

After a long moment, Cassie laughed. "Of course I know, and it's wonderful!" she exclaimed. "I *love* seeing girls work together. Please come in!"

Soon the friends were seated with Cassie in a comfortable room. "So, you really liked our presentation?" Mia asked.

"Absolutely." Cassie smiled. "Your teamwork is exactly what I try to promote on my show. I can't wait to welcome all of you on *Girl Power*."

"We can't wait, either!" Andrea said. "I'm just glad Olivia came up with the idea to work together."

"Us, too!" the others cried.

Cassie chuckled. "See what I mean? There's nothing as special as friends."

"You can say that again." Olivia smiled. "The best friends ever."